XANDER
AND THE
RAINBOW-BARFING
UNICORNS

Xander and the Rainbow-Barfing Unicorns is published by
Stone Arch Books
a Capstone imprint
1710 Roe Crest Drive
North Mankato, Minnesota 56003
www.mycapstone.com

Cataloging-in-Publication Data is available on the Library
of Congress website.
ISBN 978-1-4965-7828-0 (library binding)
ISBN 978-1-4965-8015-3 (paperback)
ISBN 978-1-4965-7831-0 (eBook PDF)

Summary: The Rainbow-Barfing Unicorn virus hasn't
infected humans . . . until now! In this adventure,
twelve-year-old Xander contracts the mysterious virus of
the Rainbow-Barfing Unicorns. The virus gives the unicorns
their barfing abilities, but it's having the opposite effect on
Xander—it's draining him of any color at all!

Designer: Heidi Thompson
Production Specialist: Katy LaVigne

Printed and bound in the USA.
2211

by Matthew K. Manning

illustrated by Joey Ellis

WHO TURNED OFF THE COLORS?

STONE ARCH BOOKS
a capstone imprint

LEGEND SAYS . . .

The Rainbow-Barfing Unicorns
come from a faraway, magical
world called Pegasia. Not so long
ago, these stinky, zombielike,
upchucking creatures were
banished to Earth for being,
well . . . stinky, zombielike,
upchucking creatures. However,
Earth presents them with a new
danger: humans.

So, just who are the Rainbow-Barfing
Unicorns . . . ?

CHAPTER ONE

Mount Ashe looked angry on this particular Saturday. Not someone-ate-the-last-brownie angry. More like, I-shall-soon-belch-lava-all-over-your-puny-town angry. It wasn't a good sign for Xander Stone's weekly magic show.

Xander could see the rather cranky mountain from the performance stage.

This was the part of his Rainbow-Barfing Unicorn magic show where the three zombie unicorns—Cradie, Blep, and Ronk—would walk through the crowd.

With fresh makeup and a spritz of hairspray, the unicorns could skip right in front visitors without anyone suspecting they were undead unicorns from the magical dimension of Pegasia. To the audience, the Rainbow-Barfing Unicorns were just miniature ponies in costumes, rigged to barf fake rainbows at the show's finale. No one suspected that they were looking at zombie unicorns in disguise, talking animals that would barf actual rainbows if they ate anything other than garbage.

The problem was that during this part of the show, the Rainbow-Barfing Unicorns weren't sheltered under the stage's slanted roof. They were out among the crowd.

The storm giving Mount Ashe its angry appearance was an actual danger to Xander's friends. Not only would the audience be caught in the downpour, but so would the Rainbow-Barfing Unicorns. If their stage makeup washed off, their real identities would be revealed. And if that happened, authorities would surely haul them off to some government lab, secret medical center, or worse.

"Ladies and gentlemen," Xander said as he stepped off the stage, "we're having a bit of a weather issue." Just as Xander finished his sentence, a large raindrop splashed down on his nose.

"Boo!" came a roar from the audience.

The visitors didn't come all the way to the Montgomery Apple Orchard to pick apples or smell the stench of the neighboring Henderson Landfill. They had come here to see Xander's show—and they weren't going to leave until they saw some magic.

"Um, well . . ." Xander began. "We're going to have to postpone—"

"Boo!" the audience roared again.

Then—*CRACK!*—a sudden crack of thunder boomed from behind Mount Ashe. A shadow fell over Xander's stage.

Xander looked up to see nothing but dark, cloudy skies. Then a few more raindrops smacked him in the face.

"—the show due to rain," Xander finished his sentence. "But we'll have another performance tomorrow afternoon at—"

"We wanna see the rainbows!" shouted an angry man, who looked a little too old to be at a magic unicorn show.

Xander looked at the Rainbow-Barfing Unicorns. Dozens of raindrops were landing on them now. Xander could even see a bit of Cradie's faded purple hide underneath her now splotchy makeup.

"OK, OK," Xander said. He now sounded less like the ringmaster of a professional stage show and more like a panicked sixth grader.

Xander rushed over to Cradie, Blep, and Ronk. He pulled out three sticks of licorice from his pocket and attempted to hand one to each of his unicorn friends. When Ronk ate all three pieces in one gulp, Xander rolled his eyes. Then he reached into his pocket for the spare licorice he already knew he'd need. This wasn't his first unicorn rodeo, after all. Most everything that could go wrong in his magic show had gone wrong in countless past performances. He had a backup plan for everything. Well, everything except for a crowd that would rather sit in the pouring rain than see their show canceled.

Xander handed Blep a new piece of licorice and then passed one to Cradle. Each unicorn quickly gobbled up the candy.

Xander examined Blep as he chewed. The unicorn's makeup was dripping to the ground below him. Xander only hoped the audience couldn't see the Rainbow-Barfing Unicorns clearly through the pouring rain.

"And now, the moment you've all been waiting for!" Xander shouted into the crowd.

He pointed to the Rainbow-Barfing
Unicorns. Right on cue, they lived up
to their rather disgusting name.

"**CRADIE!**" Cradie brayed.

"**BLEP!**" Blep shouted.

"**RONK!**" Ronk ronked.

A beautiful beam of multi-colored
light burst from each unicorn's
mouth. The beams shot through
the air, piercing through
the pouring rain.

"Woo-hoo!" The audience stood and cheered.

Xander smiled and bowed with delight.

But when Xander glanced back at the Rainbow-Barfing Unicorns, his smile quickly vanished. The unicorns' makeup had almost completely washed away!

Xander rushed his friends off the stage and across the orchard's field. They knew they couldn't afford to be spotted without their makeup.

"That was a close one!" Xander said when they got to the unicorns' stables.

The Rainbow-Barfing Unicorns started to laugh.

And though Xander knew the situation could've been serious, he laughed too.

CHAPTER TWO

By morning, the sun returned. Dozens of puddles remained on the ground, especially in the patch of earth behind the Rainbow-Barfing Unicorns' stable. Depending on the time of day, Cradie, Blep, and Ronk liked to rest in that patch and enjoy the shade created by the stable's shadow. It was in this shady, muddy place that Blep discovered Ronk around nine in the morning.

"RONK!"

Ronk had been ronking for the past hour. Even though Blep wasn't a morning unicorn, the sound woke him from the dirty mattress inside the stable. And if he had to be awake, then at least he could yell at his friend. Yelling was one of the small pleasures Blep enjoyed in life.

"What's with all the racket?" Blep yelled.

"Ronk," Ronk explained calmly.

Since Blep had no idea what "ronk" meant, he walked over to his fellow unicorn and inspected the scene himself. Ronk had been munching on a pack of cookies he'd gotten from who knows where. ("Who knows where" was the usual source for all of Ronk's mysterious possessions.) It looked like the zombie unicorn was trying to barf a rainbow at the moment.

"**RONK!**" Actually, he wasn't trying to barf a rainbow—he was succeeding at it!

Usually when Rainbow-Barfing Unicorns barfed, they barfed into the air. The beautiful beam would light up the sky, creating quite the spectacle. It was no wonder people flocked to their show at the orchard every weekend.

Today, Ronk wasn't projecting light into the sky. He was aiming his mouth downward, toward one of the mud puddles in the shady patch. The rainbow shot from out behind his crooked teeth and into the water. But instead of disappearing, as rainbows do, the colors stayed! The mud puddle itself had become a beautiful swirling pool of every color in the spectrum.

"Whoa!" Blep gasped, despite himself.

(He didn't mean to compliment his friend's work. After all, he still had more yelling to do.)

"Ronk," Ronk agreed, nodding his head. When Ronk's head shook up and down, Blep could hear something rattling around inside.

"How long does it stay like that?" Blep asked.

"Ronk," Ronk explained. The response meant nothing to Blep, but that was to be expected.

Ronk nodded his head toward the rest of the shady area, so Blep turned around. Behind him were dozens of rainbow-colored puddles. They were obviously the work of his friend's many morning ronks.

"Nice," Blep said, again accidentally complimenting the strange green unicorn.

Ronk smiled his crooked smile. He was proud of his accomplishments. He had made art—or at least a type of barfy art.

"Wow!" Cradie said as she rounded the corner of the stable. She had already noticed the puddles. "That's amazing!" she said to Ronk.

Ronk's smile widened.

"What a cool trick," Cradie said. "Don't let Xander see. He'll want to put that talent into our act."

That idea seemed to excite Ronk. Now he wasn't just a brilliant barf-artist, he was also a show designer!

"Wonder how long the puddles will stay like that?" Blep said.

CHAPTER THREE

Three hours later, the Rainbow-Barfing Unicorns were still wondering. . . .

In fact, they had been so occupied by the rainbow-swirling puddles, they nearly missed their next stage show. The audience had already been gathering in the nearby bleachers. The show would begin in less than thirty minutes—at noon sharp!

Strangely enough, Xander was nowhere to be found.

"He's never late," Cradie said to Blep as the two wandered over to their "clubhouse" at the Henderson Landfill. They lovingly referred to the area as Barf Central, which contained a few couches, splintered coffee tables, a beanbag chair, and plenty of garbage to snack on.

"Ri row!" said Blep.

At the moment, Blep could barely speak. He had a paintbrush in his mouth and was doing his best to cover Cradie's faded purple skin with a thick coat of stage makeup. The job was usually Xander's, since he had two hands and absolutely zero hooves.

"It's just unlike him," said Cradie. "We can't have a show without our announcer."

"Ronk," Ronk agreed. He was bouncing on the nearby trampoline. Some of his makeup was already flaking off. Cradie and Blep weren't nearly the artist Xander was.

Blep finished the coat of paint-like makeup. He took a step back to admire his work. He wished he hadn't. Cradie looked like a child's crude drawing of a unicorn, complete with splotchy coloring. Somehow, Blep had managed to color outside the lines in real life.

Blep spit out the paintbrush in his mouth. "We're gonna need to find him," he said. "Let's go to his house."

"OK," Cradie said. She knew Blep didn't worry very often. "But how are we going to get there?"

Hitchhiking is never a good idea—who knows what kind of weirdo might offer a ride. And that's if you're human! Hitchhiking is an even worse idea if you happen to be a Rainbow-Barfing Unicorn. But that didn't stop Cradie, Blep, and Ronk from trying.

The Rainbow-Barfing Unicorns stood on the side of the road near the entrance to the Montgomery Apple Orchard. They had immediately attracted attention. People would take one look at their poorly applied stage makeup and drive away.

To make matters worse, the Rainbow-Barfing Unicorns obviously didn't have thumbs. How were they expected to bum a ride when they couldn't even stick out the one digit known to attract drivers?

Trying to hitchhike without a thumb was like trying to use roller skates without human feet. And Cradie knew what she was talking about. She had tried both of those things.

After an hour with no luck, Cradie, Blep, and Ronk decided that their best bet was to walk, even though that would take the better part of the day at their pace. (Or at Ronk's pace, anyway. He got distracted easily.)

However, as soon as they approached the first stop sign in the road, the Rainbow-Barfing Unicorns finally got lucky. In front of them was a large pickup truck. The driver was busy playing with his cell phone, which explained why he was stopped longer than usual.

"Come on!" Cradie whispered to Blep and Ronk as soon as she realized the opportunity.

Cradie rushed over to the truck, reared back, and then leaped directly into the truck bed. Her hooves barely made a sound. She crouched down in the back, so as not to be caught in the driver's rearview mirror.

"Huh," said Blep, impressed.

Not to be outdone, Blep reared back as well. He jumped right into the bed, nearly crashing into Cradie. His leap wasn't quite as graceful as hers, but it got the job done.

Outside the truck, Ronk paced around. The strange unicorn knew he couldn't jump as far as Cradie—or even Blep—but he didn't want to lose his friends.

Ronk took a step back. Just then, he noticed the truck's brake lights were no longer glowing red. The driver was about to pull away! (Even Ronk's scattered brain could figure out that much.)

"C'mon, Ronk!" whispered Blep from the truck.

The truck slowly rolled forward.

Ronk looked both ways, as if he was about to cross a street. Then he ran toward the truck and jumped. . . .

WHAM! Ronk's front hooves were the only part of him that made the leap successfully. Blep and Cradie saw their fellow unicorn holding onto the truck bed for dear life as the vehicle turned a corner.

CHOMP! Blep bit onto one of Ronk's hooves. *CHOMP!* Cradie bit onto the other.

They pulled as hard as they could. Ronk's back legs scraped against truck's tailgate. The green unicorn tried desperately to find a foothold—or a hoofhold, as it were. Cradie and Blep pulled harder.

Finally the trio felt themselves flying toward the front of the truck bed. They slammed into the back of the cab. It hurt, but Ronk was with them. They had managed to pull him out of harm's way!

Cradie, Ronk, and Blep remained crouched down and out of sight. They were all smiling, relieved to see Ronk safe.

Then Cradie felt something between her teeth. It tasted like a . . . gummy bear? It must have been stuck to Ronk's hoof. She swallowed it before even thinking twice. After all, when it comes to sweet treats, Rainbow-Barfing Unicorns don't have the greatest willpower.

As the truck drove down a hill toward Xander's suburb, a bright rainbow shot out of its bed.

CHAPTER FOUR

A short ride later, Cradie popped her head up. She recognized the tall evergreen trees that lined the road near Xander's suburban home.

Cradie smacked Blep with her hoof. The hit was a little harder than she had intended.

"Hey!" Blep said.

"Jump!" was all Cradie said in response.

Then Cradie leaped out of the truck. Her hooves clunked against the asphalt of the road. Ronk followed without hesitation. Blep stole a glance at the driver of the truck, who was busy looking at his phone. (It was a distinctly human sickness.) Blep shrugged and then followed the other Rainbow-Barfing Unicorns.

The three unicorns trotted through the neighborhood. Cradie remembered the way well enough. She had ridden here several times in Xander's bike trailer.

After turning onto a side street, the Rainbow-Barfing Unicorns found what they were looking for: Xander's little house at the base of a mountain.

When there was no sign of Xander in the front yard, the Rainbow-Barfing Unicorns tried the backyard. No Xander there, either. Cradie was beginning to worry that they'd passed him when they were huddled in the back of the truck. But her friends weren't ready to give up the search just yet. At the moment, both Blep and Ronk were pressing their entire faces against the back door, peering inside to Xander's kitchen.

"Guys!" shouted Cradie. "They'll see you!"

"Ain't that the point?" Blep said without moving.

"It's fine if it's Xander," said Cradie. "But we don't want to have to explain to his parents how we came all this way on our own."

"We'll just let Ronk explain it for us," said Blep.

"Ronk," Ronk agreed. (That would also be his explanation, if pressed.)

Cradie rolled her eyes, but then curiosity got the better of her. She rushed over to the door, and added her face to the stack currently crowding its window.

"There!" said Cradie. She nodded toward the living room.

The room was barely visible through the kitchen doorway. But the backs of two adult heads could be seen peeking out from behind the couch. From the looks of it, Xander's parents were either watching TV or reading. Cradie couldn't be positive which.

"That's just the parents," said Blep.

"Right," said Cradie. "So where's Xander?"

"Ronk," suggested Ronk. (It wasn't the worst idea in the world.)

"Ronk's right," said Blep. He didn't understand what his friend had said, but he at least wanted to let him participate. "I think we should check Xander's room."

"Upstairs?" Cradie asked.

"Ronk," Ronk added.

Blep looked up at the roof. Then he said, "Too bad none of us is a Pegasus."

The garage door was open, and the ladder was inside. But that didn't make it any easier to carry. None of the unicorns could lift the ladder by themselves. When Ronk tried, the whole thing started to tip over. Cradie and Blep tried to dodge it, but the ladder fell right over their heads.

Suddenly, all three of the Rainbow-Barfing Unicorns looked more like Santa's reindeer than their usual selves. They were connected by the wooden "reins" of the ladder, each with his or her head through a hole between the rungs. As they couldn't look any more ridiculous, thanks to the awful stage makeup jobs they still sported, the Rainbow-Barfing Unicorns decided to just go with it. They walked around the house to the backyard. The ladder rode with them.

With a lot of effort, the Rainbow-Barfing Unicorns propped the ladder against the house with a thud. Cradie peeked through the back door. Xander's parents hadn't heard the noise. Or if they had, they didn't think much of it.

Cradie hurried back to her friends. Blep was already halfway up the ladder.

"Careful," Cradie said.

Blep didn't answer. He was concentrating.

Climbing a ladder is a tricky thing for unicorns. They can't exactly grip the rungs with their hooves. They can hold on a little bit with their teeth, but the slightest wrong move is disaster. And since Ronk didn't feel like waiting for Blep to finish his climb, if Blep fell, he'd take his friend down with him.

Finally, Blep's hooves touched the rooftop, and for the second time in as many minutes, he felt like one of Santa's reindeer. "I'm OK," he called down to his friends.

At the same time, Ronk decided he was in a hurry. The green unicorn jumped and skipped the last few ladder rungs, barely clearing the house's rain gutter.

"Ronk!" he said. His green face looked a little paler than normal.

"You never did like heights," said Blep.

Ronk was too busy shaking to respond. Some of the dust and grime flaked off of him and onto the shingles at his feet. Blep took a few steps back. He wasn't much cleaner than his fellow Rainbow-Barfing Unicorns, but he felt he should at least try to be.

"Oof," said Cradie. She had climbed the ladder in a hurry, although not quite as quickly as Ronk. She either was nervous about slipping, or wanted to make sure she didn't miss anything by being the last to arrive.

"So where's his room?" asked Blep. He was looking around the slope of the roof. There were no windows on this side.

Cradie walked past him and onto the opposite slope. From that point of view, she could see a small raised section of the house. At its end was a single window.

43

That was it—Xander's room!

Cradie was the first to look through the window. She was back in leader mode now. It was a natural fit for her.

"I see—" she began.

"What?" said Blep. He pressed his nose against the glass over Cradie's shoulder.

"It's Xander," said Cradie. "But he's . . ." She couldn't bring herself to finish the sentence.

Inside the room, Xander lay in the bottom bunk of his bed. He had a comic book in his hands but looked like he was about to doze off to sleep. His eyes were barely open.

Even though comics usually entertained Xander more than any other form of entertainment, that wasn't the strange thing about him at the moment. Xander didn't look like his usual, colorful self. In fact, his skin was gray. His hair was a darker gray. Even his clothing was gray!

"He's . . . he looks like an old black-and-white TV show!" Cradie exclaimed.

CHAPTER FIVE

"Hey, champ," Blep said as he slid Xander's window open. He tried to step into Xander's room, but instead ran into the window's screen.

Xander jolted up in bed. He had almost been asleep. He wasn't sure if he was dreaming or if there were really three zombie Rainbow-Barfing Unicorns standing on his roof.

After a few seconds, he said, "Blep?"

Blep was rubbing his newly injured nose with his hoof. "Yeah?" he said. "I hate your window."

"Hold on!" Xander said. He was using a loud whisper now, suddenly aware of the situation. He jumped out of bed. He wasn't wearing much clothing. Just a gray T-shirt and a black pair of boxer shorts. But he was too worried to be embarrassed.

Xander clicked the metal tabs at the top and the bottom of the screen. Then he pulled the screen inward and set it on the carpet in his room.

Blep jumped down into Xander's bedroom. He looked around and nodded. "Nice place," he said.

"How did you guys get here?" Xander asked, ignoring Blep's compliment.

"More importantly, what is going on with your . . . coloring?" Cradie said as she landed on Xander's carpet with a muffled thud.

"Shh!" Xander said. "I don't want my parents to come up here."

"So explain why ya look like the picture on that TV set Ronk found under a pile of cheese at the dump," said Blep.

"He means, why are you in black and white?" Cradie explains.

"I . . . ," Xander paused. "I'm not sure. If I had to guess, I'd say it's because of you."

"Me?" asked Cradie, insulted.

"Ronk," Ronk said as he fell through

the window into the room. His thump was decidedly louder than Cradie's had been.

"Well, not you in particular," whispered Xander. "All three of you."

"Gonna have to explain that one," said Blep.

"Mom and Dad, they already took me to the doctor this morning," Xander said. "Once they saw how I had lost my colors. And they're not sure what's wrong with me. Well, not exactly."

"OK," said Blep, slumping down onto Xander's bed. Xander briefly wondered if his sheets would stink once Blep got up again. He knew the answer was yes.

"Well, they know one thing," said Xander. "They know I have a virus. A virus they've never seen before."

"An alien virus," Cradie said quietly.

"I think it's the same one that turned you guys into zombies," said Xander.

Everyone was quiet for a few moments.

"Ronk," said Ronk in a sad little bray.

No one disagreed.

CHAPTER SIX

"Everything OK up there, buddy?"
Xander's dad called from the bottom of
the staircase.

Xander's eyes went wide. "Hide," he
whispered. "You can't let my parents
see you."

"Buddy?" Xander's dad called again.

"I'm fine, Dad!" Xander yelled in the
direction of his closed bedroom door. His

voice sounded anything but fine. So it came as no surprise to anyone in the room when they heard his dad's footsteps on the stairs below.

"Hide," Xander whispered again.

Ronk crammed himself under the bed and Blep followed. Cradie tried to do the same, but there just wasn't enough room.

"The closet!" Xander said in a panicked voice.

Cradie sprinted to the closet, but the door was closed. She tried the handle with her teeth, but couldn't pull hard enough.

Xander was in no position to help her either. He was in bed pulling his blankets over himself. He needed to look as sick and innocent as possible. After all, sick kids never have three Rainbow-Barfing Unicorns hidden in their rooms.

The doorknob turned.

The door creaked.

Xander's eyes darted from it to Cradie, who stood frozen near the closet. Cradie scanned the room. There was nowhere to hide, so she ran directly at Xander's bedroom door.

"Hey, kiddo," Xander's dad said as the door started opening.

WHUMP! The door suddenly stopped. Xander's dad furrowed his brow behind his thick glasses. "Huh?" he said, squeezing into the room.

"Hey, Dad!" said Xander excitedly. He sounded like he hadn't seen his father for a good month or two—certainly not just earlier this afternoon. "Look at this!"

Xander's dad gave up thinking about the

door and walked over to his son's bunk bed. Wedged between the door and the wall, Cradie let out a tiny breath. She was doing her best not to make a sound.

"What you got there?" Xander's dad asked as he sat down near Xander.

"This awesome comic book!" said Xander. His distraction seemed to be working. He held up the comic in his hands and pushed it into his dad's face.

"You feeling OK, son?" asked his dad.

"Sure!" said Xander. "I mean, I'm black and white, but otherwise, I'm OK."

"Your comic book is upside down."

"Oh," said Xander. "Yeah, I like reading them that way. It makes the stories more exciting."

"Exciting?" his dad wondered aloud.

"Yeah, not only do they have to fight the bad guy, but they have to do it while hanging from the ceiling!" Xander said. He was making this all up. He wasn't even making sense to himself.

"Right," said his dad.

"How will they do it? How will they defy gravity and the odds?!" Xander was shouting now. He had doubled down on his ridiculous excuse. He was hoping his dad would interrupt him soon. Somebody needed to stop this, that was for sure!

"I think you need to get some sleep," said his dad. "The doctor wants to see you tomorrow afternoon. Your mom had the hardest time convincing him to even let us take you home. That means you need to take it easy."

"I'm kind of hungry," Xander said.

"Yeah? How about I order us a cheese pizza?"

"Too spicy," Xander replied.

His dad looked at him. Like every kid in America, Xander had never turned down pizza. And since when was a plain cheese pizza spicy?

"Maybe I'll just have some crust?" added Xander after thinking it over.

"Ronk," said Ronk from beneath the bed.

"What was that?" Xander's dad asked.

"I said 'OK,'" said Xander.

"It sounded like you said 'Ronk,'" said Xander's dad.

"I added too many letters to it," said Xander.

Xander's dad wasn't really listening to his son at this point. He was busy smelling the air. He gave Xander a suspicious look. Finally, he stood up and said, "We need to change your sheets soon."

Xander just looked at him.

"It stinks in here," his dad said. He patted Xander on the head and walked out of the room, closing the door behind him.

Cradie collapsed to the floor. She was exhausted from pressing herself as flat as possible against the wall. "Take a little longer next time, why don't you?" she joked.

"Sorry, I—" Xander started to say when Blep interrupted him.

"Did you see his feet?" Blep said.

"Whose feet?" asked Xander.

"Your pop's, kid," said Blep. He slid out from under the bed. "We could see 'em as clear as day from under there."

"What are you talking about?" asked Xander.

"Your dad was walking around barefoot," said Blep.

"Yeah, so?" Xander didn't understand.

"His feet were gray, Xander," said Blep. "He's turning black and white too."

CHAPTER SEVEN

Xander immediately leaped out of bed! He sprinted to the window and slid down the ladder. As they had discovered earlier, the Rainbow-Barfing Unicorns weren't meant to travel via ladder. Cradie, Blep, and Ronk took nearly twice as long to get down.

But once Xander's feet touched the grass, he still showed no signs of slowing down.

"Xander!" Cradie called after him as she followed him to the street.

As soon as Cradie had yelled, she realized it was a mistake. It would be bad enough if someone saw her chasing after Xander so far away from her stable at the Montgomery Orchard. That would be pretty difficult to explain. It would be way worse if someone actually heard her speak. There'd be no explanation for that situation.

In either case, Xander didn't answer. He just kept running away from his house farther down the street. Cradie kept galloping after him.

"Ronk!" she heard behind her.

Cradie glanced backward and could see both Blep and Ronk following. They looked to be gaining on her, despite the fact that Ronk was running in a zigzag pattern. She hoped her rather odd unicorn friend didn't run into a mailbox—or worst yet, one of Xander's neighbors!

Xander neared the end of his street and turned. Cradie rolled her eyes. Exactly how much running was this day going to include?

As it turned out, not much more . . .

When Cradie rounded the corner, she nearly ran smackdab into her human friend. Xander had stopped at the edge of a yard and was staring at a house Cradie recognized. They had been there before. In fact, this was where the Rainbow-Barfing Unicorns had made their public debut as show "ponies." This was the house of the girl

Xander had a crush on. This was where his friend Kelly lived.

"Xander!" Cradie whispered.

He didn't reply.

"What are we doing here?" Cradie continued.

Xander was out of breath. That was clear. He was huffing and puffing so much, it was like he just realized right this second that he had been running. So again, he didn't respond. But to be fair, he would have been lucky to squeeze a single word out in the state he was in.

Cradie heard a noise coming from behind Kelly's house. Without hesitating, she dove behind a nearby hedge. Xander stood frozen in his tracks. He was a black-and-white statue, as if sculpted by an artist.

"Xander!" Cradie whispered.

The statue didn't move. The voices behind the house got louder. Cradie was pretty sure Xander didn't want his entire neighborhood seeing him in black and white. So she jumped back up. She dug her unicorn horn right underneath his shoe's laces, and then pulled her friend down to the ground.

After she had pulled Xander back behind the hedge with her, the boy finally spoke. "Thanks," he whispered, through a few huffs and puffs.

"Come into the sunlight where I can get a better look at you," came a familiar voice from nearby.

It was Kelly's Aunt Melinda, the owner of the Montgomery Apple Orchard.

Cradie wasn't sure why Aunt Melinda was in Xander's neighborhood and not at work. But when she and Kelly stepped into the sunlight near the front of the house, it all became obvious.

"What is happening to us?" Kelly asked her aunt. Her eyes were big and a little wet. She looked extremely worried.

Cradie thought she had every right to be. Because both Aunt Melinda and Kelly had lost their color!

"This is all my fault," Xander whispered.

Cradie looked at her black-and-white friend and then back at the two other gray-toned humans near the house. She knew the boy was wrong. It wasn't his fault.

The blame fell squarely on her own shoulders.

CHAPTER EIGHT

The closet in Xander's basement seemed smaller than the last time they had used it. Blep, Cradie, and Ronk all rested there on the ground, on the horrible One Trick Pony cartoon sheets that Xander claimed belonged to his sister. The more Cradie thought about it, the more she had her doubts. Someone had clearly written "Property of Xander" on the pillow's tag.

The Rainbow-Barfing Unicorns had been hiding out in Xander's basement since the day before. It had been raining again for the last few hours of the morning. Even if Xander wanted to risk being seen in black and white out in public, he certainly wasn't willing to bike all the way to Henderson in the downpour.

"There's got to be a solution somewhere," Xander said.

"There's gotta be a bigger closet somewhere," Blep joked.

Xander ignored him and paced the closet.

"All this pacing and worrying isn't going to solve anything," said Cradie. "Let's just relax." Thinking about Aunt Melinda's office, Cradie added, "Don't you have a TV down here?"

Television was quite a treat for the Rainbow-Barfing Unicorns. They didn't have such a thing on Pegasia, and they certainly didn't have a set in their stable at the orchard. If nothing else, Cradie knew the TV would do wonders for calming her own nerves. A good distraction might even help Xander.

Xander thought it over. "Hold on," he said, exiting the closet.

He was gone for what seemed like an hour to Cradie. Blep was complaining, Ronk was moaning, and she was feeling a little cramped in the tight space. (In reality, Xander was gone for less than three minutes.)

When Xander returned, he carried a large box nearly half his size. It was a television set, Cradie realized upon further inspection.

It just wasn't the type of flat screen TV Xander's parents enjoyed upstairs in their living room. This dusty old thing looked to be state of the art . . . back in 1987.

A large orange cord trailed from the back of the TV. "I plugged in the extension over behind the washing machine," Xander said to the Rainbow-Barfing Unicorn, as if those words meant anything to magical unicorns from Pegasia.

"Great," said Blep. He didn't seem to mean it.

Xander pushed a button underneath the dusty screen, and then wiped the dust away as best he could. He made three clean stripes across the length of the set until he gave up the effort and found a seat on the floor near Ronk.

Ronk dropped his head onto Xander's lap. Xander sighed. There went another pair of perfectly clean shorts. They were now coated in zombie unicorn filth. Oh well. He wasn't really a fan of gray clothing anyway.

The television buzzed to life. Cradie watched as a picture formed on the screen seemingly out of nowhere. Even on this hulking outdated machine, TV was magical to a unicorn.

". . . eye on your neighborhood. Channel 4 News begins now!" the TV was saying.

"Great," said Xander. "The news." He sighed again. Cradie was surprised how much Xander sounded like Blep at the moment.

"Then change the channel already," said Blep.

"Can't," Xander responded without looking at his friend. "This thing only gets one channel."

"We begin this morning with breaking news from Henderson," said the blonde newscaster. For some reason she was smiling. It seemed inappropriate to Cradie, but then again, she wasn't a professional newsperson. "A strange presumed virus that effects pigment, and oddly enough, clothing, has caused a rash of sickness in the area, with reports of the illness stretching as far as many surrounding cities."

"Oh no," Xander said under his breath.

"We now go live to Corey Hughes in downtown Henderson," said the woman.

The image changed to a young man standing downtown, holding an umbrella.

Strangely enough, it didn't seem to be raining any longer. A few people could be seen talking on the sidewalk in the background.

"Look at them!" Xander said. He leaned forward toward the TV and tapped on the screen, hard. "There!"

Cradie squinted. It was hard to see in the less-than-ideal picture of the old television set, but Xander was right to be so worried. All the people milling about in the background were in black and white while the reporter was most definitely in color. The people in the background seemed to be munching on something from a large brown sack. Cradie at first thought they might be eating raw potatoes, but that didn't make any sense.

"I can't believe it's spreading like this!" Xander said.

"I can," said Blep. "I mean, think about it. How many people have we entertained with our 'magic' show? Some of 'em got plenty close to us. Just makes sense they caught the virus if it's contagious to humans."

Xander turned around and looked at Blep.

"Well the good news is," Cradie said through a broken smile, "at least it stopped raining."

Xander examined the TV. The reporter was lowering his umbrella as he talked.

"OK," Xander finally said after thinking for a few minutes. "Let's get you guys back to the farm."

Blep, Cradie, and Ronk all stood up. Ronk stretched.

Then he shook out his mane. Mud, hair, and what looked like a half-eaten lollypop now decorated the room.

"But first, I'm gonna need to make a stop in the kitchen for breakfast," Xander said.

"Sounds good to me," said Blep. "Could you grab us something too?"

"Sure," said Xander. "How do you feel about boiled beets?"

CHAPTER NINE

Xander and the Rainbow-Barfing
Unicorns sat in the woods behind his
house, sharing a plate of boiled beets. The
Rainbow-Barfing Unicorns had never tried
beets before, yet they were certain that
Xander had overcooked them.

"Are these supposed to have, like, I don't
know . . . flavor?" Blep asked. Then he
turned his head to the side. "Blep!" he called

as a rainbow burst through the woods and
into the otherwise gray sky.

Xander didn't answer. He had a beet in
his hand, eating it like an apple.

"Butter would do wonders for these," said
Cradie, before adding, "Cradie!" Another
rainbow ripped through the tree line.

"Ronk!" Ronk agreed. His was both a
response and a rainbow eruption.

Xander was too busy working on his fifth beet to think anything of it.

"Seriously," said Blep. He walked away from his half-eaten beet and found a nice, partially dry rock to sit on. "What's next, boiled potatoes? Or how about some equally flavorless poi to liven things up?"

Xander finally took a break from furiously devouring his breakfast. "Do you have any boiled potatoes?" he asked. His eyes were wide with excitement.

Cradie and Blep exchanged looks.

"How about your favorite?" said Cradie. "A nice tart green apple."

"The virus did come with cravings," Blep said to Cradie. He was talking to her like Xander wasn't even there. The way Xander was chomping on his sixth beet, he might as well not have been.

"But boiled potatoes?" Cradie said.

"Do you have any boiled potatoes?" Xander repeated, more anxious and excited than last time.

"Um, no," Cradie was saying. But Xander wasn't listening. He had darted out of the woods and was already at his house's back door.

"This is bad," Blep said, watching the black-and-white boy dash inside.

Cradie exhaled loudly. She looked at Blep with concern. Then she glanced over at Ronk. He didn't seem particularly worried at the moment. In fact, he was smiling. IIe had found a puddle the perfect size for his continued experiments.

"Ronk!" he brayed as a rainbow shot from his mouth into the muddy water. As before, the rainbow stayed in place in the shallow pool. It glimmered in the shadows of the trees, like a magical—yet disgusting—oasis.

Cradie sighed even louder. Then she heard a scream from inside Xander's house.

"Yes!" a woman's voice exclaimed. "That's a great idea!"

Just that second, Xander raced back out the door and into the little forest.

"It's a go!" he yelled as he got closer. He stumbled into the tree line again, saying, "Mom's making boiled potatoes right this second! She's super excited about it!"

"Is she black and white too?" Cradie asked.

"Huh?" said Xander. Then he added, "You know, I didn't notice."

Blep stepped forward, about to speak. But unfortunately, at that exact moment, Xander began pacing again, looking back at Cradie as he walked.

"I can't wait until we—" Xander began. But he never finished his sentence.

Instead, Xander tripped over Blep's back and stumbled toward Ronk. Ronk jumped out of the way, clearing the path so Xander landed face first into the newly formed rainbow puddle.

"Xander!" Cradie yelled.

"Ronk," Ronk said in a sad little voice. He had worked very hard on that particular piece of "artwork."

Xander leaned backward and shook his head, splattering rainbow-dyed drops of water on several nearby trees. "I'm OK," he said after catching his breath.

"You're more than OK," Cradie said out a now-gaping mouth.

Blep cracked his aching back and then peered up at Xander. "Whoa," he said quietly.

"What?" Xander said.

The Rainbow-Barfing Unicorns were too amazed to tell the boy that his colors were back!

CHAPTER TEN

The tires on the bike's trailer squeaked as Xander wheeled through downtown Henderson. He had gotten a little too tired of peddling the weight of the three zombie unicorns hiding under a blanket in the trailer. About ten minutes ago, he'd hopped off his seat and was now taking a break as he pushed his bike down the sidewalk.

He had successfully regained his breath.

But that wasn't what he was worried about. Xander was hoping no one in the town realized that he was the only person who had any color at all.

On his right, two black-and-white women wearing drab, gray police uniforms were arguing over something. Xander couldn't tell what it was without steering his bike closer to them, an action he was not willing to take.

To Xander's right, three gray-toned kids were snacking on raw beets. They seemed as happy as if they had just flagged down an ice cream truck. Xander shuddered. His belly still ached from all the boiled beets he had devoured earlier. Now that he had regained his coloring, he wasn't anti-beet, he just thought they should either be buttered or pickled if they meant for people to eat them.

The cravings he had suffered while sick with the alien virus were gone. Now he wanted nothing more than a tall glass of lemonade. Very flavorful lemonade, if possible.

"*Psst* . . ." Blep whispered from under the blanket. "How's it looking out there?"

"Bad," Xander said, not bothering to whisper. As it turned out, no one was paying him any attention. All downtown Henderson cared about were beets and potatoes. Well, Xander had overheard one old gray-toned man talking about stale saltine crackers with no salt. Xander wondered if those should just be called "tines."

"Cradie's got an idea," Blep whispered.

At that, Xander wheeled the bike toward a patch of unoccupied grass at the start of the small city park. There, in the shade of a tree and safely away from any beet-obsessed townspeople, Xander could talk freely with the Rainbow-Barfing Unicorns without anyone overhearing them.

"OK," said Xander. "What's the plan?"

Cradie popped her head out of the blanket. "The reservoir," she said. "We fill up the city's water supply with rainbows. That way we can cure the whole town in one swoop."

"OK," Xander said again. "So where's the reservoir?"

"I don't know," said Cradie. "You're the human."

"Won't they have, like, security there?" Xander asked.

"Probably," said Cradie.

"So how do we get past them?" Xander asked. "I mean, I'm a sixth grader and you're three Rainbow-Barfing Unicorns."

"You're making this plan sound difficult," said Cradie. She wasn't happy that Xander was pooping this particular party.

"Because I think it is difficult," he said.

Cradie hung her head.

"Hey, you got any better ideas?" Blep asked. He stuck his head out from under the blanket as well. The blanket fell behind the trio of unicorns and into the grass.

Xander looked around. No one was noticing these unicorns with their all-but-wiped-off stage makeup. The only humans around were an elderly couple gnawing on raw potatoes. The old man seemed to be having the roughest go of it. He removed his potato from his mouth, and his set of dentures came out with it. His wife frowned at him.

Xander shrugged. There didn't seem to be a point in hiding his unicorn friends any longer.

Which was fortunate, because Ronk had no intention of staying hidden. The unstable unicorn jumped out of the back of the trailer and trotted over to one of the park's metal grill stands. Xander and the rest of the Rainbow-Barfing Unicorns watched the unicorn with curious expressions.

"Ronk," Xander said. "Come on. Get back here. We don't have time to play."

But Ronk wasn't interested in playing. He leaned down and gripped the pole-like base of the grill with his broken teeth. Then he shook it vigorously. Gray ash instantly coated Ronk and the grass around him. As if he had just solved all the world's problems, Ronk strolled proudly back to Xander, Cradie, and Blep. He smiled his crooked smile and waited for a response.

"What is wrong with you?" Xander said. "It's going to take forever to hose you off."

"Too bad it's not raining anymore," Blep said, almost to himself.

Then Cradie's eyes went wide. She looked from Blep to Xander. "That's what Ronk's trying to say!" she almost shouted.

"Ronk," Ronk said. He gave a knowing nod.

"Ashe," said Xander. As if prompted, thunder cracked in the distance. Xander titled his head toward the towering mountain beyond the town. Another huge storm cloud was forming behind it. "Mount Ashe," Xander said, finally getting it.

"We don't need to rainbow the water supply," said Cradie. "We need to rainbow the clouds themselves."

Xander and all three Rainbow-Barfing Unicorns looked toward the intimidating mountain.

"Ronk," Ronk said in a quiet voice.

CHAPTER ELEVEN

Xander and the Rainbow-Barfing Unicorns had gone as far as the road could take them. He looked up, but there wasn't much to see. Just a stretch of forest past a wire fence that clearly read: No Trespassing. It was hard to tell they were even at the base of Mount Ashe. It was just a steep hill from this vantage point, one that showed no signs of stopping as it disappeared into cloudlike plumes of mist.

Thunder crashed, bringing Xander back to reality.

"The storm's going to pass completely if we don't get a move on," Cradie said.

She and the rest of the Rainbow-Barfing Unicorns were out of the bike's trailer now. They hadn't seen a human being other than Xander for a good fifteen minutes. Mount Ashe wasn't really a tourist attraction, so the unicorns had no fears of being discovered.

Xander wheeled his bike and trailer to a nearby ditch. They couldn't be spotted from the road there. The deep trench should serve as enough cover. He reached into the trailer and pulled out a small, roundish object. He put it in his pocket.

Better safe than sorry.

"I guess there's no turning back now," Xander said.

It was quiet there near the country road. Only the sound of a dog barking in the distance could be heard over Xander climbing the tall wire fence that separated the forest from the road. After a good five minutes of pure, out-of-shape effort, Xander had conquered the fence. He fell to its other side with a thud. He gave the concerned Rainbow-Barfing Unicorns a thumbs-up from his position on the ground.

Cradie was next. With a scuttling of hooves and rotten teeth, she made her way up the fence. She leaped gracefully down to the ground near Xander. Blep did the same.

But when they looked for Ronk to see if he was following, there was no sign of the weird little green unicorn.

"Ronk!" came a voice directly behind Xander. He jumped, before realizing who it was that was ronking. It's not like the list of suspects was very long.

"How did you—" Xander began as his eyes drifted to the fence behind Ronk. There he saw a Ronk-size hole cut neatly in the wiring. It was as if it had been eaten away by a particularly odd zombie unicorn. "Oh," Xander said under his breath. "Great." He was going to have to send a check to whoever owned this property.

Xander was already uneasy about the idea of trespassing. But property damage was too much for him. He wondered how many weeks of Rainbow-Barfing Unicorns shows it would take to pay for a new section of wire fencing.

Without another word, Xander and his friends began to hike up the mountain and into the forest. They were all too nervous to notice that the sound of the barking dog was getting louder.

CHAPTER TWELVE

"Stop right there!" shouted a deep voice from the woods.

Xander and the Rainbow-Barfing Unicorns had been walking for the better part of an hour when they heard the man yelling at them. The young boy certainly didn't expect to see any other hikers this far up the mountain.

Xander turned to see a man armed with a shovel. The shovel seemed an odd accessory, but Xander didn't think much about it in the heat of the moment. Behind the man was a very large brown dog. The beast seemed as big as a full-grown horse. It wasn't, but don't try telling Xander that.

"Um . . . hello?" Xander said.

"What the Sam Hill are you doing up on my property?" asked the man. Xander didn't know who Sam Hill was. He was in no hurry to find out.

"Just . . . just out for a walk," said Xander.

"Not up here you ain't," said the man. Now Xander was really confused. Of course they were. The man could see them for himself. This was exactly where they were walking. "You go on and get."

"Oh, uh, sure," said Xander. "But we were kind of hoping to reach the top of the mountain first, if that's not a problem." For the first time, Xander realized that this man was in black and white. It was hard to tell at first. Gray tones seemed to be a natural fit for this old-fashioned character.

"We?" said the man. "Who's we? There more of you kids out here?"

Xander realized he had been talking about his unicorns as if they were people, not ponies in costumes, as he wanted others to believe. One minute into a conversation, and he was already blowing his friends' secret identities.

"No," said Xander. "I misspoke. It's just me. Me and my . . . um, ponies."

"Enough blabbering, then," said the man. "Off my land. Now." There was no maybe in this man's voice. He was giving a direct order.

Xander locked eyes with Cradie. This wasn't going to work.

"And here you were worried about guards at the reservoir," she whispered.

Then, without another word, she ran full speed at the strange man.

Using her horn, Cradie knocked the shovel right out of the man's hand. He yelped in surprise more than pain, but it was enough to anger his dog. The dog began barking at Cradie. Blep and Ronk rushed over to their friend, but the dog didn't back down. He snarled and showed his sharp fangs.

So the Rainbow-Barfing Unicorns did the same. They opened their mouths, revealing their rotten—and in some cases missing altogether—cracked teeth. It might have been the sight of their unseemly chompers, or perhaps their breath, but something spooked the dog. He yelped louder than his master and then turned and ran away.

Unfortunately, the man wasn't as easily frightened. He picked up his shovel again and swung it at Cradie. She barely dodged the attack, narrowly escaping with her horn and head intact. He swung again at Blep. Blep leaped out of the way but collided with Ronk and Cradie in the process. All three unicorns fell to the ground, dazed.

The man stood over them. He raised his shovel for a final blow. And then something hit him square in the forehead.

The man looked at the ground through hazy eyes. As soon as they regained their focus, he could see that there was a raw beet lying on the grass near his work boots. His mouth fell open. His hands fell to his sides. The shovel fell to the ground with a harmless thunk. Then the man pounced on the beet and began to chew it madly like a wolf that had chanced upon a T-bone steak.

"Wha . . . ?" Blep said as he got to his hooves.

"Let's go!" shouted Xander. In no time at all, he and the Rainbow-Barfing Unicorns were rushing through the woods toward the mountain's peak.

CHAPTER THIRTEEN

Xander reached into his pocket. He was out of beets, but had the next best thing, gummy worms. He threw one to Ronk, one to Blep, and one to Cradie. They swallowed the gooey candy without even chewing. Then they titled their heads toward the massing rainclouds above.

"You can do it, guys," Xander said. He felt a raindrop land on his nose. Then another on his arm. "It's now or never," he added.

Three beams of beautiful, multicolored light lit up the air there at the top of Mount Ashe. The light shot from the rock formation where the Rainbow-Barfing Unicorns stood into the huge gray clouds over their heads. The three rainbows hung in the sky. Beautiful, disgusting barf rainbows. Then they faded from view.

No one said anything for a few seconds.

Then Cradie broke the silence. "Did we do it?" she asked Xander.

"I don't know," Xander said.

As if in reply, another raindrop landed on him. Then another. Then another. Xander raised the back of his hand to his face. There, swirling and shimmering near his knuckles, were a few pools of water with a rainbow trapped neatly inside. Xander held out both of his hands. The rain was coming down heavier now. It took no time at all for him to catch a few more raindrops. Each was multicolored and beautiful. He looked over at his unicorn friends, but they were busy splashing and playing in the rainbow rain.

■ ■ ■

The news of the cure to the black and white virus traveled quickly. An old couple had been caught in the rainstorm in downtown Henderson, and regained their color in a matter of seconds. Before Xander and the Rainbow-Barfing Unicorns had even gotten back to their stable at the Montgomery Apple Orchard and Farm, the citizens of every town in a forty mile radius were out dancing in the street, making a rainbow mess of their clothing and shoes. As he sat in Aunt Melinda's office, watching her TV set, Xander was sure the crisis had been averted. Their cure had worked.

BREAKING NEWS

He and the Rainbow-Barfing Unicorns walked through the pouring rainbow rain back toward the Henderson Landfill. The Rainbow-Barfing Unicorns were hungry after their adventure, and needed a spot of garbage-supper to tide them over until the next day. Blep and Ronk ran ahead, anticipating their dinner. But Cradie kept pace with Xander. She had something to say to him. Xander could tell that just by looking at her face. Unicorns were never good about keeping feelings to themselves.

"What's up?" he said when the other two unicorns were out of earshot.

"Nothing," she said. But then thought better of it. "I just don't get it," she said.

"Get what?"

"Well, we're the reason for the color loss,

right? In the humans? I mean, we brought that alien virus here," she said.

"Yeah," said Xander. "Probably, I guess."

"So if it was the same virus, then how come the rainbow rain didn't cure us too?"

Xander stopped in his tracks. He hadn't thought about that. Of course Cradie would want to be cured. No one can enjoy being a zombie. Were there any perks in a life of barfing rainbows?

"I don't know," said Xander. "But it obviously affected humans in a different way. Maybe it was a mutant strand or something that only worked on people. It's not like the virus ever hurt any other unicorns you guys knew in Pegasia."

Cradie hung her head low. "Yeah," she said. "Probably something like that," she said.

"I'm sorry, Cradie," Xander said.

The two walked through the gate to the Henderson Landfill. Before Cradie could say anything else, Ronk splashed a puddle of rainbow-colored water at her face. She wiped the rain off. She still looked upset.

"Oh," said Blep. "Um . . . sorry about that."

Cradie's eyes narrowed, her nose crinkled. A slight smile appeared in the far corner of her mouth.

"It's on now!" she said before braying something not unlike a happy war cry.

Cradie charged at Blep, knocking him into a huge rainbow puddle. Xander opened his mouth to say something, but that was indeed a terrible idea. Because in the next instant, Xander was spitting out a mouthful of rainbow water, trying his best to stop laughing.

CHARACTER SPOTLIGHT:
XANDER!

Height: 5 feet, 5 inches

Species: Human

Home Planet: Earth

Horn Length: N/A

Xander Stone is an average sixth grader. Well, actually, he WAS an average sixth grader . . . until he met the Rainbow-Barfing Unicorns. Now he's an average sixth grader with the responsibility of keeping Blep, Cradie, and Ronk a secret from pretty much all other humans. Or the fate of the world could be at stake. No biggie.

GLOSSARY

banish (BAN-ish)—to send someone away from a place and order them not to return

contagious (kuhn-TAY-jes)—able to be passed on by contact between individuals

dimension (duh-MEN-shuhn)—a place in space and time

distraction (dis-TRAK-shuhn)—something that makes it hard to pay attention

landfill (LAND-fil)—a system of trash and garbage disposal in which the waste is buried between layers of earth

reservoir (REZ-uh-vwor)— an artificial or natural lake where water is collected as a water supply

spectrum (SPEK-truhm)—the range of colors shown when light shines through water or a prism

BARF WORDS

blow chunks (BLOW CHUHNGKS)—to barf

heave (HEEV)—to barf

hork (HORK)—to barf

hurl (HURL)—to barf

puke (PEWK)—to barf

ralph (RALF)—to barf

regurgitate (ree-GUR-juh-tate)—to barf

retch (RECH)—to barf

spew (SPYU)—to barf

throw up (THROH UHP)—to barf

upchuck (UHP-chuhk)—to barf

vomit (VOM-it)—to barf

yak (YAK)—to barf

JOKES!!

What's black and white and
eats like a unicorn?

A zebra.

What kind of bow is
easiest for a Rainbow-
Barfing unicorn to tie?

A rain-bow!

Why was the
unicorn such a good
guitar player?

He knew the
uni-chords.

Do they have unicorns at the zoo?

Yes! They're just large, gray, and called rhinos.

Why can you always trust what a unicorn says?

They're no bull.

How do you know that a unicorn has been in your house?

There's glitter everywhere!

AUTHOR

The author of over seventy-five books, Matthew K. Manning has written dozens of comic books as well, including the hit *Batman/ Teenage Mutant Ninja Turtles Adventures* miniseries. Currently the writer of the new IDW comic book series *Rise of the Teenage Mutant Ninja Turtles*, Manning has also written comics starring Batman, Wonder Woman, Spider-Man, the Justice League, the Looney Tunes, and Scooby-Doo. He currently resides in Asheville, North Carolina, with his wife, Dorothy, and their two daughters, Lillian and Gwendolyn.

ILLUSTRATOR

Joey Ellis lives and works in Charlotte, North Carolina, with his wife, Erin, and two sons. Joey writes and draws for books, magazines, comics, games, big companies, small companies, and everything else in between.